A NIGHT AT THE DINER

CAMERON PENDLETON

ILLUSTRATED BY
DEMETRE WILLIAMS

BALBOA.PRESS
A DIVISION OF HAY HOUSE

Balboa Press books may be ordered through booksellers or by contacting:

Balboa Press
A Division of Hay House
1663 Liberty Drive
Bloomington, IN 47403
www.balboapress.com
844-682-1282

Because of the dynamic nature of the Internet, any web addresses or
links contained in this book may have changed since publication and
may no longer be valid. The views expressed in this work are solely those
of the author and do not necessarily reflect the views of the publisher,
and the publisher hereby disclaims any responsibility for them.

The author of this book does not dispense medical advice or prescribe the use
of any technique as a form of treatment for physical, emotional, or medical
problems without the advice of a physician, either directly or indirectly. The
intent of the author is only to offer information of a general nature to help
you in your quest for emotional and spiritual well-being. In the event you use
any of the information in this book for yourself, which is your constitutional
right, the author and the publisher assume no responsibility for your actions.

Any people depicted in stock imagery provided by Getty Images are
models, and such images are being used for illustrative purposes only.
Certain stock imagery © Getty Images.

Print information available on the last page.

ISBN: 978-1-9822-6749-0 (sc)
ISBN: 978-1-9822-6750-6 (e)

Balboa Press rev. date: 04/14/2021

SECTION 1

CONTENTS

I

6:00 A.M.

Every morning soon after the break of dawn, I wake up to begin my morning at Scarlett's Southside Diner. Located at 3320 Lakeview Ave in Los Angeles, California. My brisk morning walk entices my anticipation because I know a few of my favorite things are waiting to greet me. Scarlett's diner is lavishly decorated combined with low lighting at certain times of night for romantic reasons. The diner is located in a great neighborhood, the people are friendly, and the waitresses are always aesthetic pleasing to look at.

Every morning, as a creature of habit I order the same thing, a vanilla bean frappuccino topped with whipped cream and caramel. The waitresses here know my order by memory and as I walk into the doors, I'm greeted with a smile as they tell me my order is coming right up.

My mouth watered like a faucet as I watched the waitress sit my vice down on the table in front of me. I almost stroked out, but not from the Frappuccino.

My pupils locked onto her pretty brown iris as she whispered for me to enjoy, with a coy smile on her lush lips. I replied I sure will, but didn't touch my beverage until she walked away. I had to take a second to admire such a flower.

INTIMACY

Having no one to love, you find yourself making love to your words. She watches them roll off my tongue, but "intimacy" never left her plushy lips.

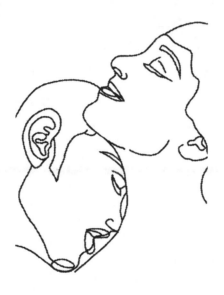

A LETTER FROM MY THOUGHTS

Dear Me….

It's your thoughts again, I just have a couple questions that I want to ask you.

What is life without love? Exhausting & dull. What is a heart without blood? So exanimate. What are lungs without oxygen? Just a pair of deflated balloons if you ask me. What are you doing with your life?... Huh? Why you keep coming to this diner when you know that none of these waitresses have interest in you… why?

You know love goes over your head every chance it gets. You know it could be you & a couple of your friends hanging out together & every last one of them would take someone home except you. Why keep trying? Every time you reach for the stars you fall right on your face all over again. How many times does that have to happen for you to realize that there is nobody for you? How many times do you have to break your own heart just to see someone happy that you should have left alone a long time ago? I tell you every single day! To leave that girl alone & what you do? Go right back to her knowing that you're still going to get the same results as last time… let it go!

Your such an imbecile you repeat the same steps over & over again. You push everyone away!. Just because a flower wants to be your friend does not mean you should detach it from the ground, take it home, & keep it as if it was yours. I can't believe you and you wonder why you never had any luck with flowers. You incompetent being when will you ever learn.

DEAR BEAUTIFUL WAITRESS

Dear Beautiful Waitress

Your eyes are bright and dreamy like a starry night. Your skin is silky and smooth as if you were made of milk and honey. Your hair texture is like a cloud on a cloudy day if only I could run my fingers through it. Your smile is bright as the sun and Your perfume is so fruity and aromatic.

You're my Excedrin that I digest when I get migraines.

You're my umbrella that shields me from the pouring rain.

I've noticed you, but you never acknowledged me or even know that I exist. That's okay though I can just cherish you in my mind until the day comes when I finally have the guts to approach you. To be honest I may never reach that point, but as long as I have this letter it'll make me feel better.

I find it strange that I know nothing about you, but I'm so in love with you. All I know is that you're a waitress at my favorite diner and that you're always working when I'm here. You're all that I see I can't even finish my delectable beverage without fantasizing about you and our future.

I want to know all your likes & dislikes? What makes you laugh? and what makes you cry? I want to know what keeps you alive. Is it alcohol? Is it weed? What motivates you to get up every day and hustle the way you do? I also want to know if you have a special someone.

Can you just walk up to my table and ask to take my order already? So I can stop drowning in my thoughts.

It's just something about you. you stand out to me.

I have thoughts of buying you flowers, but I'm not sure which flowers you would like and if you would like them coming from me.

Yeah…never mind I rather not.

Sincerely,
Your Secret Admirer

MYOCARDIUM

Nothing hurts more than giving someone a chamber of your myocardium and it still isn't enough. Remember to only give a portion of yourself to someone. I rather them break a portion of me than to demolish my entire heart, At least I won't have much to replace.

Never put your all into anyone until they show you they're worth it. You never want to give 1000% to someone just for them to say they only want to be friends. Unless you enjoy the feeling of being deceased internally.

It hurts accepting the fact that certain characters in your story are over. Try not to beat yourself up about it just replace the old characters with new characters. There is no need to hold onto expired people.

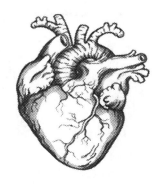

FIRST IMPRESSION

Looking out my peripheral I saw the waitress making her way to my table to take my order.

My hands stiffened as if I was diagnosed with rigor mortis, the circuit breaker in my brain malfunctioned. I was prepared to push her away.

"Hello sir, I will be taking your order this morning. what can I get for you"? the waitress said with a professional smile.

Umm…May I have a sausage, egg and cheese sandwich on wheat toast. Could you also apply butter to my toast, along with an order of your world famous home-fries? She replied, "No problem coming right up!". There goes my last drop of oxygenated blood in my myocardium. At least I had a chance to speak with her before I went into cardiac arrest.

Excuse me waitress! I said, waving my arms carelessly as if I saw a long lost friend.

Yes? the waitress said.

What is your name? I said anxiously not knowing what her response would be.

"Thalia" she said with an unsure look on her face.

I'm Aiden… Aiden Viotto I said. She replied "Hi" with a forced smile as she made her way back to the counter.

Maybe she's not interested. I'll keep trying.

OVERANALYZE

I can guarantee her interest in me is lower than my self-esteem.

Maybe she'll be flattered by my intentions, but when it comes to dating me I wouldn't be an option.

Maybe she'll love the feelings I have bottled up inside and wouldn't mind if I pour them onto her as if my emotions were tepid water. Just for her to retreat and act accordingly. Do you consider this a waste?

Take a moment and think about it. She's beautiful, very cordial, well put together, and then there's me. An addict for a star that's beyond my scope.

It amazes me how a single thought can place you in such a dreadful mood.

Overanalyzing something is such a curse. I wouldn't wish my mind on my worst enemy. In my head I'm either digging too deep or barely scratching the surface.

I FALL IN LOVE 2 EASILY

I fall in love way too easily. For a person with a heart that breaks like annealed glass I should be more careful with who I give my heart too.

But I'm never careful.

A regular smile, a simple compliment, a conversation where u show interest in the topic I'm speaking about... I fall in love almost instantly.

A warm hug and 30 seconds of attention is more than enough to wrap me around your phalanges like an adhesive bandage.

I hate being this way, but my heart is in control.

TELL ME HOW YOU FEEL

Tell me how you feel... that's what she always says, but whenever I pursed my lips and leaned 80 degrees in her direction I always plummet.

I believe words are uncalled for when you constantly express how you feel through your actions. Is that not crucial? Actions are much more raw and powerful sorta like poetry just in physical form.

I looked her in the iris and inhaled deeply before rising to perform my presentation. My physician never diagnosed me with anxiety, but before I spoke I felt my tongue twist and the words in my brain vanish. If only I knew sooner that my words could push you farther away from me than you already were I would have kept my mouth glued shut.

Tell me how you feel?

FOOD FOR THOUGHT

(She's coming back be cool Aiden… Please be cool).

"Here you go Mr. Viotto" she said, with a reassuring smile. I guess she could read the anxiety that was written all over my face.

I replied thank you so much and don't call me Mr. Viotto, just call me Aiden.

She replied, "Okay Aiden enjoy". I replied thank you and found myself starring at her circular gelatinous buttocks as she walked away. Not only does my 3rd leg fill with fluids whenever I see a delightful gluteus maximus, but also when she smiles at me after leaving my table.

DESPONDENCY

Nothing hurts more than losing hope within yourself.

Nothing hurts more than knowing that no one wants to love me.

Nothing hurts more than knowing that love leaps over my head every chance it gets.

Nothing hurts more than falling for someone that's unavailable.

Nothing hurts more than coming home to my room every day and not seeing someone waiting for my arrival.

Nothing hurts more than having to swallow how you feel when your around someone you find so appealing.

Nothing hurts more than watching no good people receive what I deserve.

CLOSING TIME

The saddest part of the day is closing time. All the customers are leaving, and the waitresses are cleaning up and gathering their things to head on home.

I stayed at my table and told every waitress that tried to make me leave that I was "waiting for someone"

This was my chance to finally ask Thalia out on a date.

About 2 minutes after I was told to leave the diner here comes Thalia headed towards the door.

She looked so different in her street clothes I just could not take my eyes off of her.

Hey! Wait up. I said while speed walking to the door

"Hey Aiden, your still here?" Thalia said curiously.

Yes i didn't leave because I wanted to ask you something. I said nervously.

"Ask me what"? Thalia said looking a bit anxious.

I was wondering if we could hang out sometime and get to know each other a little more. I said scratching my head.

"Yeah sure I'm free Friday night are you available"? Thalia said.

Of course I'm available! I replied with a huge smile.

"Great! There is a restaurant downtown called "le Tore's" I can meet you there friday night at 8:00 P.M"? Thalia said with a gentle smile.

That sounds great! I said.

"Okay see you then" Thalia said while walking out of the door".

The biggest smile appeared on my face as I watched Thalia walk out of the diner. I said to myself "finally it's my turn to be in love". Finding love is like trying to win the lottery. There's a 20% chance of winning and an 80% chance of you getting the wrong numbers.

PURCHASE

You ever wish you could purchase love?

All because the more you search for it the farther it moves away from you. It's much easier to just purchase love and bliss instead of struggling to find it. Feel free to call me a dunce, for chasing something that only exist in movies. My feet are sore because I've been running for years and I've gone through several boxes of band aids and many other adhesive bandages. They say love is pure, so I search barefooted to feel each and every pebble and cooled tar between my toes and on my soles along the way. But I think it's time to slow down. I think it's time to stop completely.

The more you think about how bad you want something or somebody that you have yet to have the less it interests you. When you're crushing on someone it may take months or even years before you approach them and when it's time to finally approach them you've lost interest already.

Running after somebody that doesn't give you a chance to catch up. they just keep running & running and they never stop to take a breather.

So why keep pursuing them?

LE TORE'S

Tonight is the night.

(Don't fuck this up).

I'm so nervous right now. My hands are soaked, my legs are shaking, It feels like someone is stabbing me in the abdomen, and My mind won't stop racing. I don't know what to do with myself.

I wonder what she will be wearing. I didn't know what to wear myself, so I rented a black peak lapel tuxedo. Hopefully she thinks I'm handsome. I know I supposed to feel good about myself, but it doesn't hurt to get approval from someone else… right?

Le Tore's restaurant is a great place to take a special someone. Waiters are well mannered, appetizers are endless, and the lighting is dim and romantic. Can't forget about the lit candles in the center of the table between you and the love of your life. I can't believe it. I never thought I would ever go on a date again.

The clock struck 8:00pm still no sign of Thalia.

What if she stood me up?

What if this was all a joke?

My brain started revving up to prepare itself for the race until I saw a woman in a beautiful black dress walk into the restaurant.

It was Thalia! I think it's safe to decrease the pressure on my brain accelerator now.

She looked so beautiful and dissimilar in her dress.

Thalia over here. I whispered to avoid drawing attention to myself.

"Hey Aiden, you look... amazing wow I'm so used to you being in street clothes I didn't know you could clean up so nice". She said with a face I had never seen her make before.

Thank you Thalia. You look very stunning yourself. I said confidently.

I'm sorry! where are my manners allow me to get your chair for you. I said getting up from the table.

"Why, thank you Aiden! you're such a gentleman" she said.

"So tell me about yourself". Thalia said

Well you already know my name is Aiden Viotto. I am 25 years of age. I am a salesman at "Bill & Locke Paper Company". Actually it's not far from here only a couple blocks away. I've been working there for about 5 years now and I'm in the process of becoming assistant regional manager. I am also a poet and been working on my anthology for about 2 years. How about yourself?

"That's so awesome! If you don't mind I would like to read some of your work one day. My name is Thalia Rose. I'm 23 years old. I'll be 24 in July. I am a waitress as you already know. I'm also in college to become a criminal defense lawyer. I've been working at Scarlett's diner for 3 years now and I love it. Even though working at a diner isn't my dream job, but it'll help pay off my college debt.

Of course! you can read some of my work one day and wow! A criminal defense lawyer that's awesome.

What inspired you to become a lawyer? I said smiling from ear to ear.

"Great"! Thalia said with a huge smile staring into my soul. I've always found law fascinating. Lawyers also make a good amount of money so that definitely motivated me as well.

"Tell me about your personality"? Thalia said.

I would say I'm on the lines of introversion. Because I can be a bit shy and reticent. I'm more so of a homebody then a guy that likes to go out drinking at night clubs with the guys. I can be inane as well and that'll forever be a part of me. As a child my family called me "Goofball" because I legit laughed at almost everything. I personally don't think being an introvert is exciting, but the world made me this way, but it also has it's perks at times. Overall I think that I'm a nice person. Anyway enough about me what is your personality like?

"I'm more of an extrovert. I'm very outgoing and I enjoy being around people that I love. I go to clubs with my girlfriends from time to time, but not to pick up guys or anything I just go for a drink and a good time. I consider myself fun to be around no one has ever complained about the energy that I release into the atmosphere". Thalia said.

My thoughts began to talk over me. I said to myself maybe this won't work after all. I'm an introvert and she's an extrovert. I can already picture the restless nights up thinking about what she's doing while she's at the club with her girlfriends. Nowadays "girlfriends" are bad influences. Always preying on that one friend that actually enjoys being in love with one man at a time.

That's awesome it sounds like you have a beautiful soul! I said with a forced smile.

She replied, "Thank you! so do you!"

I replied Thank you! and took a gulp of my alcoholic beverage.

"Ahem! Sir and Madam the main course is ready" the waitress said in a fancy accent.

I ordered Le Tore's world famous Escargot and Thalia ordered their delicious Filet De Boeuf.

"Bon Appétit" the waitress said before making his way to the next table.

How is your "Filet De Boeuf"? is it what you expected? I said while slurping the escargots out of its shell.

"It's great I never had filet de boeuf before." Thalia said.

We both finished our dinner and our conversations so we decided that we should call it a night. I walked Thalia to her car to make sure she remained safe like a gentleman should. But I also did something that I regret.

"Thank you so much for tonight I really needed some time away from home" Thalia said.

No problem at all. Are we going to hang out again? or was this only a one time thing? I said.

"Yes we can hang out again whenever we're both available." Thalia said.

Okay sounds good. I said.

Listen… Thalia I adore you so much. You're the only person that crosses my mind without looking both ways. You never use caution and I love that about you. You're fearless, open minded, and overall a bewitching soul. You're the only reason why I come to Scarlett's Diner every single day. I know for a fact that if you were to quit today I would never go to that diner again. I know I haven't known you very long, but this gut feeling that I've been feeling all night with you just feels so right.

"Awe that's so sweet Aiden". Thalia said.

Thalia opened her arms and reached for a hug. Her arms wrapped around me like chains as her soft breasts pressed against my chest. Her vanilla scent was so refreshing along with her warm silky skin. It was a hug I never wanted to end. She released her arms from around my waist and started staring into my pupils as they dilated. When I leaned forward to kiss Thalia's plushy lips she immediately turned her face forcing my lips to land on her cheek.

I'm sorry! I shouldn't have done that. I said with deep remorse.

"It's okay Aiden you didn't do anything wrong. "I'm going to head on home now I could use some time alone to think things through". Thanks again for tonight" Thalia said while getting into her petite vehicle.

As I watched her drive away I felt my tendinous cords detach from my myocardium. I was left speechless on the sidewalk wondering why. Why would I do such a thing so quickly.

Was it me being desperate? probably so... I always water the soil before planting the seed.

BOTTOMLESS PIT

Learn to live your life without getting your hopes up for every little thing.

Rejection doesn't hurt as much when you don't have your hopes flying in the air to begin with.

Treat every girl or guy as if they're your friends only. Never assume anything is going to happen between you too.

If someone likes you… great! be patient though and don't move too fast. Some people don't know how to respond when under pressure.

Hold onto how you feel for as long as you possibly can. You don't want to tell him or her how you feel in just a couple of days and find out that the feelings are not going to be reciprocated.

Having your hopes up all the time you'll find yourself floating around in your mind wondering will you ever be good enough for anyone. You'll be free falling in your thoughts as if your mind is a bottomless pit.

P.S. never expect "you" from other people. It'll be times when you're giving them 90% and they're only giving you 50%. don't get upset about it either accept them for who they are or leave them alone. Simple. Just because you go out your way for them doesn't mean they'll do the same for you.

SECTION 2

CONTENTS

II

II

APOLOGIES 4 SALE

What a time to be alive! I'm glad Thalia is getting more comfortable with me but it's a little strange at the same time because why get close to me out of all people?

On the other hand, she's confusing and very hard to read I wonder why? Could she be reopening a wound that was recently stitched? Is that the reason why her signals are mixed?

Me being a road runner I tried caressing her lips with mine. Instead my lips caressed the left side of her cheek. I know… it was a terrible idea, but I just couldn't resist the urge. Her body language told me that she was interested, but I guess I misinterpreted her actions. Of course I wasn't given the response I was looking for. She used words like "that's so sweet" after I poured my feelings onto her. Her response crushed my larynx causing me to develop dysphasia.

My core began to rot. I asked myself "what should I do now"? I put so much thought and energy into this… Was it all a waste? How can I pretend to be okay when the person that occupies all of my headspace won't talk to me? I was lost. I didn't know where to look, where to go, or even how to start my day. Its mind blowing that my words changed our entire story.

When I apologized she denied I did anything wrong. She stated that she needs her space and time to think things out. Maybe I should apologize again in advance so the next time I fuck up I can save my breath.

TAINTED MIND

First thing in the morning I open my eyes and thank God for allowing me to see another day. The birds are singing, and the sun is beaming through the windows around my noir curtains hitting me directly in the face. If that isn't a wakeup call I don't know what is.

I picked up my cellular device just to see if anyone texted me "good morning". My phone read "No Notifications". Nothing to be upset about I'm pretty used to seeing that by now. 5 years and counting my notification screen has been blank. It was silly of me to even check.

Here I am scrolling my life away on Instagram drooling over women I will never have. Reading relationship posts 2 or more times because it's so relatable. Reminiscing about past toxic relationships and wishing I stayed in it just so I can feel less lonely. I kept scrolling and scrolling until the joints in my thumb stiffened.

Usually during the day I'm fine. I have plenty of things to do to help keep me busy, but once I sit down and relax my mind starts to wander. To a place that's beyond earth's atmosphere. Living with a tainted mind is a piece of work. Only time bliss is discovered is when my mind is occupied. It's a shame that I have to stay "busy" in order to feel okay. If only I could escape my own mind.

PEACE OF MIND

You want to feel free?

Let go of all the hurt in your life.

You want to feel appreciated?

Look in the mirror and tell the figure that's looking at you, "I love you". I'm sure they'll need to hear it.

You want to feel loved?

Go out and treat yourself to something nice.

Nothing in the world will ever compare to a peace of mind. Love yourself, treat yourself, appreciate yourself, and free your mind from all the hurt that life brings.

DESPERATION

2 weeks later still no sign of Thalia. I wonder if she's still breathing. Do you think she hates my guts? I wonder if I'll ever see her again.

Me being obsessive I find myself passing by the diner daily to see if Thalia is there taking orders, but she wasn't. Thalia's coworkers haven't seen her in 2 weeks either, I guess she really needed that mental break away from everybody. I feel a little better now that I know I'm not the only one she's separating herself from, but I still would like for her to return. At least come back to work I don't want her bills to overflow.

I have thoughts of blowing up her phone with calls and text messages, but I think I'll tattoo "pressed" on my forehead instead just for having that thought. Her phone is never too far away from her anyway, so I know for a fact she'll answer her phone. Maybe I can text her and tell her that "It's an emergency" and

I need to speak to her immediately. She'll reply then since it's an emergency right?

Why do I have to be so desperate?

Desperate for something that'll eventually maim me once I allow it into my life.

DIAL TONE

It was the start of the 3rd week when I finally received a phone call from Thalia. She stated, "the break was well needed", but she mentioned something to me that made me feel like I was shot in the chest with a 357 magnum. She said, "Aiden I'm sorry but I'm emotionally unavailable right now". You're a great person and I enjoy what we have already, and I don't want to mess that up. I'm sorry if my actions confused you or made you think something was about to happen between us I just wanted to be your friend".

I froze... I just couldn't get my words out. I was completely paralyzed.

10 seconds later I replied... Okay cool sounds good to me". You mind if I give you a call back? I have a ton of work to do that has to be on my boss desk by tomorrow morning.

She replied... "Sure no problem call me later."

Before she could finish her sentence I hung up immediately. My thorax began to ache, and my lungs deflated. At this very moment I knew I needed to forget about Thalia.

THE ART OF LETTING GO

It wasn't easy letting go of someone that meant so much to me in a matter of months, but it was the right thing to do. Yes, I fell on my face, but don't I always. It's a shame, but it's life... It's my life. Always have been and it may always will be.

I hate myself so of course I'm not going to discover anyone to share my heart with. You supposed to love yourself first so when that person comes into your life you both can share each other's happiness together. But I just can't. I can't love myself. I may get a haircut or wear a nice outfit from time to time, but I'll still think less of myself.

I understand you have the right to have a type and to like what you like, but I don't understand why I'm never no one's type.

I thought "intelligence" were one of Thalia's nonsexual turn ons...apparently not.

But that's okay. I'm used to the pain. Same result just a different person.

I'll survive.

PHILOPHOBIA

It's nice when you pair up with another person and can call it "love", but it's also scary because you start to ask yourself what do they want from me? Is it my money? What did I do to cause them to have interest in me? The questions I always ask them and seconds later the chair slides away from the table and she's charging to the exit full of rage because I put a stop to her evil plan. If you close shop early they're forced to go waste someone else's time.

The fear of love and intimacy can change your mindset towards everyone. You start to think every person you meet is out to hurt you. When in reality that may have been the "man" or "woman" of your dreams, but your too damaged to even realize it.

If people had labels dating would be so much easier. You would already know what you're getting yourself into before you even conversate with the person.

I've noticed the people you want are the people who will hurt you the most and the people who want you will cherish you and love you for who you are and wouldn't regret a second of it.

When will I feel comfortable enough to give my all to someone?

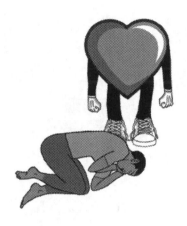

SAVE ME FROM MYSELF

I haven't been myself...I caught myself staring at my reflection in the mirror. I began to cry while my reflection taunted me. My reflection wants to end me, but no one would feel my pain if it's self-inflicted.

I find myself avoiding romantic movies, love scenes, and anything else that involves couples. I HATE IT!

"Hatred" corrupted my body systems. I couldn't eat, I couldn't sleep, I could barely breathe at times.

If only I wasn't a sponge. "Hatred" would have never seeped through my pores.

I let "hatred" get the best of me. Can you please save me from myself?

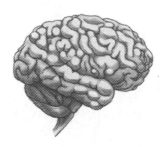

MARY DANIELS

Freshly diced broccoli pearled into chocolate flavored tobacco paper waiting to be burned.

Along with a bottle of Jack Daniels that have been sitting in my cabinet for several months now.

Mary Daniels isn't good for the brain or the liver, but she'll always make you feel so alive. The moment you take a sip or place your lips on the butt of the spliff everything disappears. All your pain, worries, unwanted weight, financial issues, etc. Everything floats away. As I watched the clouds levitate to the ceiling Mary wrapped her arms around my shoulders and whispered "how do I make you feel" so softly in my ear sending chills down my neck and making goosebumps appear.

I replied amazing! What was I mad about before Mary?

She replied "Thalia Rose, but don't worry about her. Take another sip just put me back in your mouth".

She takes you to a place that's out of this world. A place you'll never want to leave. A journey you'll never want to end.

Sadly the feeling only lasts but so long.

She's just a temporary fix.

AISLE 7

Today marks day one of me attempting to erase the thought of Thalia out of my mind and I'm already struggling. I can't even drive down the street without seeing someone with the same car as Thalia even down to the paint job. What grinds my gears is that I have to drive past "Scarlett's Diner" in order for me to go to work every morning. I find myself looking over at the diner every time I drive past wondering if I would see Thalia. I think it's time to find another way to get to work.

I know she's probably wondering why I haven't called her or maybe not. Maybe she doesn't care.

I've been running low on food at home, so I think I'll go grocery shopping today. That'll keep my mind occupied. Even though she's always on my mind like a fitted hat, but I'll try my best to stay sane.

"AJ's Supermarket" off of Violet Avenue is where I always go to purchase groceries. AJ's fruit and vegetable selection are legendary along with their reasonable prices. What you think I should cook for dinner tonight? Steak and potatoes or pepper steak with gravy over rice? I think I'll go with the steak and potatoes. Aisle 7 has all types of potatoes you can possibly think of. Russets, Sweet Potatoes, Red Potatoes, Purple Potatoes, etc. That wasn't the only thing that caught my eye in aisle 7. There was a petite woman also in aisle 7 that I couldn't take my eyes off of.

I wanted to approach her, but I was too afraid. Maybe she'll reject me just like Thalia did. I haven't had any time to recover from what just happen a couple days ago. I'm moving too fast! Oh what the hell I'm going to try anyway. ("Don't you do it you're going to regret this"). Oh shut up brain last time I checked I'm in control here not you.

Excuse me ma'am? I said while walking towards her.

"Yes" she replied.

I couldn't help but notice how beautiful you are, and I was wondering if were single by any chance?

"Sorry I have a boyfriend" the petite woman said while walking away from me.

Maybe I should have listened to my thoughts.

After being rejected I made my way to the checkout line. After completing my transaction it was time to head back home to my empty apartment.

SUBCONSCIOUS

You ever have so much to say, but can't put any of it into words? Yeah me too.

I'm conscious about a lot of things, but you'll never know it because I never speak on it.

I come home and fall asleep in an empty king size bed every night, wishing I could roll over and see a beautiful woman lying right next to me. But that'll never happen.

I usually think about things that I desire to help me fall asleep at night, but lately I've been dreaming about Thalia and I hate it.

Once she received the eviction notice stating she have to leave my cerebrum she then made herself at home in my cerebellum. But I thought you supposed to move forward not backwards.

She may skip town for a while, but she'll always remain deep in my subconscious.

EQUILIBRIUM

Maintaining balance is key in everything you do in life. Too much of anything isn't a good thing so be sure to split your time down the middle.

You'll find yourself being so focused on one thing forgetting that you had other things to do as well. Don't allow something or somebody to occupy all of your time.

Never be too self-centered. You can spend time with yourself, but hang out with your friends sometimes as well. don't be so hooked on a girl or a guy that you like you'll be so wrapped up in their life you'll forget about your own.

For instance, Aiden is so deep in Thalia's abyss to the point where he forgot he was about to become assistant regional manager. His focus was all on Thalia and not his work.

Never forget to maintain balance.

SECTION 3

CONTENTS

III

LIBIDO

I've been having trouble controlling my thoughts lately. I have a hard time keeping good eye contact with Thalia whenever she's in my presence.

A majority of the time my eyes were glued onto her perky milk bags and stunning backside. I'm not saying I didn't adore Thalia's heart, but I'm a man do you expect me to not have thoughts about intercourse?

I loved Thalia's soul as well, but I noticed as time went on my feelings for her turned off as if I was a light switch while my lust levels increased tremendously. Now when I hear her name my oral cavity waters and all I can think about is caressing her insides with my membrum virile.

Go ahead and say it "All men want is sex", but all women want is money. Are we even now? Clearly, we're both on the wrong page. Maybe we're just picking the wrong people.

Sex isn't everything so don't be a slave to your libido. If I were you, I would crave "intimacy" because it's no better feeling than making love to someone your connected to on every level.

SELF-CENTERED

Never be afraid to separate yourself from people to help improve yourself. It's all about "you" anyway. "You" are the only person that can make "you" happy. You're tired of being alone? Yeah me too, but do you love yourself? that's the question.

You can't love someone else if you don't love yourself first. Once you accomplish that goal you can now focus on building your self-esteem. Believe that you are beautiful inside and out regardless of what other people may say or think of you. Be comfortable in your own skin because you are all that you have for life.

People may call you selfish for being so self-centered, but that's okay. Those are the people that do not belong in your life. If they were your friend/ lover they would understand where you're coming from. But you have to learn to accept people for who they are, or you'll never have friends or a lover.

Once all your goals are met and you've fixed everything that needed fixing within yourself all you have to do now is wait.

A MESSAGE FROM ME 2 YOU

Let love find you. Don't go searching for it like I did and get your heart ripped into shreds. You'll only find gold diggers and expired people that just want to waste your time.

Continue to do things that you love. Pick up new hobbies, hangout with friends, or do things that you never did before. Take your mind off of love and I promise you love will come your way when you least expect it. Your soulmate could be "pushing" a door that says "pull" because they still have things to fix within themselves before they can meet you. Just be patient. Pray about it and leave it alone. Yahweh will deliver on his own time.

Don't be afraid to open up. Every person is not out to hurt you. Put yourself out there and allow yourself to get hurt so when the next person comes into your life you'll know exactly how to handle the situation better than you did before.

If you get hurt don't shut yourself down heal then move onto the next person. There are 7.8 billion people in the world trust me you will find someone else.

There is a person out there for everyone you just have to believe.

FALL IN LOVE WITH BEING ALIVE

Fall in love with being alive and stop depending on others to make you happy. Happiness is already within you so why look for it in others?

Thank Yahweh every day for allowing you to see another day. You're healthy, you have your family, you have a roof over your head, you have food on the table etc. Appreciate the things that you have, you can't miss what you never had so why put all your focus on it?

You didn't find love yet? Big deal you still have so much to live for. You have so much potential so why waste it? Enjoy every day like it's your last day on earth. Don't be down in the dumps about something that will come with time. You'll get it. It's just not your turn yet.

SELF-WORTH

Ladies and Gentlemen know your worth. That is one of the most crucial things in life. I know you may have been hurt by someone that made you change the way you view your worth, but your better than that. Trust me.

Never settle for less. If you know your worth more don't stop until you receive what you deserve.

Just because someone couldn't find it in their heart to appreciate you doesn't mean you've lost your worth. That person opened the door for someone better to come into your life. Someone that will acknowledge your worth, cherish all of your characteristics, and treat you as if you were a ruler in their kingdom. You ever think that maybe you're too good for someone? and that they're not on your level of thinking? I think you should take that into consideration.

You're worth the wait, your worth fighting for, continue putting that positivity out in the open. Oh and while you're at it grab a couple of snacks, relax and watch your heart grow.

ALTER

Regardless of what happens in life never change who you are. That is the worst mistake you will ever make.

If you're in a relationship and your partner wants you to change your ways or certain characteristics about yourself that defines you...Don't. Your soulmate was created to be compatible with you and only you so what exactly will you have to change?

A person that truly love and cares about you wouldn't want you to change anything about yourself. Even down to your flaws that's what makes you unique.

It'll be times when you think you need to change things about yourself in order to have a chance with that person you like. If you have to change yourself for someone to like you or to even acknowledge you they were never worth it in the first place. Again never forget nor question your own worth.

Depending on the situation the person may change things about themselves to adapt to you. Just so you can stay in their life. But that person will only change themselves if they can see that you're not the problem.

Going through life you will be hurt plenty of times by so many people, but don't allow those events to change who you are within. Always remain the same because one day someone will appreciate every little thing about you.

RED FLAGS

When you meet someone new make sure you look out for the red flags. As soon as you notice the red flags leave the person alone immediately! Your time is precious, and time is something you will never get back once it's wasted.

The dating stage is all about getting to know the person to see if you and that person are compatible with one another. Don't be the person that acknowledges the red flags, but continue to deal with the person just because you don't want to be alone, or you don't want to start all over again. Don't repeat my same mistakes. Sometimes starting over is the better option because everything is fresh. You start off on a clean slate that person don't know you or nothing about you and vice versa.

Take advantage of the dating stage that's the time when you ask crucial questions. Where do you see yourself in 5 years? Do you have a vehicle?, Do you have your own place or at least working towards getting your own place? Can you cook? What is your profession? and etc. Pick that person brain especially if you're the type that want to settle down and have a family, you don't want a person that's no good being the mother or father to your child.

OIL & WATER

I woke up this morning feeling like I can conquer the world, so I decided to grow a cojones and head on back down to Scarlett's Southside Diner. Not for Thalia…I just miss their frappuccino's that's all.

I jumped out of bed, did my morning routine, put on a nice outfit, made my bed up, and headed on out the door. As soon as I made it to the door I received a text message from Thalia. I was surprised she texted me, I thought she would have been done with me by now. The message said, "Hey Aiden I just wanted to check on you to see if you were okay, I hope I'm not bothering you". I decided not to reply because I was headed to the diner anyway. I thought I should pop up randomly to see her reaction.

15 mins later I finally made it to the diner's parking lot after attempting to get myself mentally prepared for what's to come. It took me about 10 or so minutes, but I'm here now so that's all that matters. I walked through the diner doors and was greeted by a waitress named Jacqueline. As she walked me to my booth she began to make conversation with me, but it was

difficult to engage due to me scanning the vicinity for Thalia. "Here is your menu sir the waitress will be over in just a moment" Jacqueline said. I replied okay thanks as she walked away from my booth. Still no sign of Thalia, maybe she's in the kitchen hiding out. I know I said I didn't come here for her, but deep down inside that was the main reason all along. A few minutes went by and there goes Thalia coming from behind the counter where I first laid eyes on her. She started speed walking to my booth until she noticed that it was me. She stood in front of me with her arms folded and said "Hello Aiden long time no see" I sensed an attitude, so I immediately cut straight to the chase. You want to know why I stop talking to you? She replied "yes" as she sat down in front of me. Because I was hurt from what you said. You told me that you were "emotionally unavailable" which didn't make any sense to me. You told me I looked "amazing" the night we went to Le Tore's, you wanted me to tell you about myself. You were actually interested in what I had to say, you even ask to read some of my work. "Yes I know I said those things Aiden, but friends do things like that all the time. Just because I wanted to learn more about you and wanted to read some of your work doesn't mean that I'm attracted to you" Thalia said looking confused. I never made it this far with someone, so I guess I just overanalyzed the whole situation.

"Yes you did Aiden, but it's okay like I said before I will love to be your friend I just don't think I'm ready to fall in love again" Thalia said getting up from the table". Watching her walk away made my heart ache, it felt as if I lost apart of myself even though she said we could still be friends.

Before she made it back to the counter another customer walked through the doors. He was a tall, muscular guy, wearing all black with a nice haircut. He greeted Thalia with a hello and a warm smile. Thalia smiled back without hesitation and then breached his personal bubble to give him a passionate welcoming hug. He then extended his neck in her direction she reciprocated his energy and their lips locked into place. My heart broke into small fragments damaging my other vital organs. I got up from the booth and started heading towards the door.

So this is why you told me your "emotionally unavailable"? you were ready for love this entire time you just didn't want to be with me. Instead of putting me through all of this bullshit you could have just told me that from the beginning and I would have never asked you on a date in the first place. "Aiden! wait" Thalia said. "what the fuck is going on here Thalia? who the hell is this guy? " the muscular guy said to Thalia while making serious eye contact. "It's a long story James". Thalia said. I attempted to leave the diner when James grabbed me by the collar and hurled me into the table booth. "James stop! He didn't do anything wrong!". Thalia said screaming at the top of her lungs. I got back on my feet, inhaled deeply and sent a flying hay maker which connected with James jawline. He didn't budge. "you're so dead" James said to me while cocking back his fist. Here comes Thalia stepping in front of his cocked back fist to stop "Bluto" from hitting me. "Get out of the way Thalia" James said aggressively. "No this needs to stop right now". Thalia said. You don't have to worry about me anymore I said while walking out of the diner.

"Aiden stop let me explain" Thalia said with regret pouring out of her pores. I don't have shit to say to you! Leave me the fuck alone! Don't call me!, don't text me!, don't even let my name cross your mind, just stay out of my fucking life! I said with no remorse.

My anger exceeded its limits. I jumped into my car and started burning rubber. Going 110 mph down a 35 mph road and not giving a single fuck.

I realized that me and Thalia are like "oil and water" we'll come in contact with each other, but we'll never mix.

IDEA OF YOU

You ever love the idea of someone? Or only love the person you created in your head? Sometimes they don't actually love you they just love the idea of you. Some people love the idea of being in a relationship and some just want someone to stick around because they're lonely. It's fucked up, but that's the way the dice rolls.

But you'll know when someone only loves the idea of you. They'll encourage you to be more of what they want you to be. Your needs won't matter as much as their needs. Your needs will never be met. Everything will be about them and only them. Your opinion will no longer matter.

IDEA OF LOVE

You ever think that you're in love with the idea of being in love? Constantly chasing a feeling that's unexplainable. A flame that only stays lit when you're with someone and once the flame goes out you're back searching for that feeling again. You tend to believe your life will be complete once you find the love of your life. You wait for someone to come into your life to make you feel happy.

Well I think I figured out the problem. I never felt the feeling of true love, so I searched for it constantly until I was left with nothing at all. Rushing into things, being addicted to the person, creating the perfect woman in my mind, attempting to change her into who I want her to be.

It all makes sense now.

DEATH'S DOOR

I can't believe Thalia kissed another man right in front of my face like that, she couldn't wait until I left the restaurant. I can see I didn't mean shit to her after all. I made it to freeway 101 now going 130 mph on a 60 mph highway and I don't plan on slowing down. But I'll try calming down because it's plenty of fish in the sea. I shouldn't let one girl alter my perspective on love. Only thing is that she was a special fish.

After about 5 mins of talking to myself I decided to slow down. I placed my foot on my brake pedal and nothing happened. On the 2nd attempt I applied more pressure to the brake pedal and the car still wouldn't slow down! I pulled my emergency break; my tires began to screech and I immediately loss control of the car. I then collided with 2 other vehicles that was also traveling north on Freeway 101. My car flipped into the air and the moment I hit the concrete…

News Reporter: *Silence…Thank you John this is Valerie Moore from Channel 5 News reporting live on scene of a fatal car collision on Freeway 101 in Los Angeles, California. We appear to have 3 vehicles involved in the collision, 2 civilians were able to walk away alive, but sadly we have 1 fatality. At this time there are no information on how the collision happened, so until further notice I am Valerie Moore with Channel 5 news back to you John…*Silence.

John Miller: Thank you Valerie and it is so sad to hear about another fatality from a motor vehicle collision I will be sending my deepest condolences to the individual loved ones.

SECTION 4

BONUS

IV

DEAR AIDEN

Dear Aiden,

Yahweh speaking, what happen son? You were so close to finding your true love. I was just adding the finishing touches to her personality just so she can match yours perfectly. She was exactly what you needed to help you better yourself in life, but you let Lucy catch up to you. You were so stuck on Thalia when she wasn't even worth it in the first place. I knew all along, but it was up to you to figure it out yourself. I can see now that I should have held your hand through this process, but you were too deep. You were no longer swimming; you were beginning to drown. I'm sure you questioned my existence, but never spoke on it and it's okay, but you have to realize that things happen for a reason. Sometimes you put things upon yourself and have the nerve to look up in the sky and ask, "why me Yahweh"?

I'm sorry your life had to end so soon, but all u had to do was forget about Thalia and patiently wait for the person I had made just for you to come into your life. Thalia now will realize how much you really meant to her, but it's always after the soul leaves it's shell to crossover into the afterlife. Now she will never know how much of a great person you were Aiden. They never realize what they have until it's gone forever and then will wish they treated you differently when you were alive. I just wish you has seen the red flags when I saw them.

Sincerely,
Yahweh

PURCHASE LOVE II

To answer your question Aiden, no I do not wish I could purchase love. You shouldn't allow something like that to even cross your mind. Why would you pay for something that will come to you in time and free of charge? I know you want love in your life and want to be loved by someone other than your family, but it isn't your time. The more you keep asking and begging for it is just going to make me take my time even more son. It's still things you need to fix within yourself before you can meet the love of your life. For now, continue being happy by yourself. Enjoy your own company, focus on work, your hobbies, etc. I promise son she's coming you just have to be patient. Stop hunting for it all your doing is hurting yourself son. If every woman you talk to rejects, you or the relationship starts off well and then ends suddenly that is me telling you it's not your time and to focus on yourself. Trust me she's waiting for you as well. Just trust in me and I will deliver when the time is right.

DESPONDENCY II

Son the one thing you should always keep in tack is yourself. Never lose yourself, especially over something that can't be controlled. Son your young, you have decades ahead of you to find someone to love. Everything you're going through right now is for a reason. The best advice I can give you is to let it happen. You have to remember good people always finish last. So let all the bad people have their time because once it's your turn to love it'll be forever.

I FALL IN LOVE 2 EASILY II

I knew exactly what I was doing when I created you son. I gave you a big heart for a reason because the world is in need of people like you. It's not too many people in the world that's like you and that's fine that makes you rare. You come from the same tree as others, but just a different branch.

I created you to be a loving, caring, and humble individual. It doesn't take much to make you happy. You're not materialistic at all, you take what is given to you and you cherish it forever. You are a very simple person, simply spending a day with you will make your entire week.

The little things a woman does to you makes you fall in love. My other children would say you lacked some sort of love in your childhood, but really your heart is just bigger than your body.

DAILY DEPRESSION II

Your mind isn't tainted Aiden. I know you struggle with being alone, but you're going to be fine. You complain about not having notifications when you first wake up in the morning, but it's okay it's not mandatory nor guaranteed. You watch videos of couples on social media to keep from losing hope in love, but you also hate watching them because it makes you feel even more lonely. You say, "you're drooling over woman you'll never have", but you fail to realize the ones you want will hurt you before the ones you need. Stop going after the girls that are "gorgeous" and start giving the decent girls a chance. They just might be the best thing that has ever happened to you, but you'll pass her up to have that "gorgeous" girl that'll cheat on you and treat you like garbage all at the same time. Your alone for a reason, you can look at it as me protecting you from all of these toxic women. If I didn't care I would have let every girl that you wanted a relationship with hurt you, but instead I made them do things you didn't like to help free you up for the woman of your dreams. I know it hurts now but you'll thank me later.

PHILOPHOBIA II

You will feel it in your soul when you finally found the one. It'll be a feeling that's inexplicable. Wherever you go it'll feel like home as long as that person is by your side. You'll know when you can give your all to that person, but until you find that person continue to only give a portion of yourself to protect your heart and mind. Expect nothing to happen between you and that person. Let things flow and eventually you'll find out that person's true intentions. Never fear nor shut love out of your life because you need it. It doesn't matter if its family love or romantic love. Since you can't have romantic love right now cherish your family and yourself. That could be the key as to why your still alone.

SAVE ME FROM MYSELF II

Sounds like Lucy is getting the best of you. You're letting "love" drive you crazy my son. Now your thoughts are taunting you and telling you to commit suicide. Do you wish for eternal suffering? I don't want you doing something that you're going to regret once it's done. Take life day by day my child, if Lucy whispers things in your ear don't listen. Don't give it that satisfaction that it wants. Lucy wants you to fail, Lucy wants you to harm yourself, Lucy wants you to do the wrong things fight it my child fight it!

OIL AND WATER II

I'm afraid you put this on yourself Aiden. You were told by Thalia herself and were given the signs that she was not available, but you continued to chase after her anyway. Did it ever cross your mind that maybe I had something to do with it? Maybe I was the one that blocked her from being a part of your life. You are so hardheaded why won't you trust in me Aiden? That's your problem you move too fast, you don't take your time, and you don't leave things alone when you can clearly see nothing is going to come out of the situation. It's good that you don't give up as easy, but somethings you need to just put an end to... Let her go.

DEATH'S DOOR II

My son never fight over a woman. I've created so many beautiful women why stress over this one person. Once again you let "love" get to your head and you were not thinking about how fast you were driving. Now you're unconscious in a ditch on freeway 101. Your ribs are broken from hitting the steering wheel, your head and your mouth won't stop bleeding, and you're breathing isn't adequate enough to sustain life. All of this because you saw Thalia kissing James. I hope you learned you're lesson my son. If you never decided to go back to the diner to see Thalia, you would still be alive right now. You allowed love to kill you my son why? Why do you want romantic love so badly. There is so much more to life then love Aiden.

Aiden my son you have to promise me something before I allow you to have a 2nd chance on Earth. Promise me you will stop chasing woman that is not worth your time. Promise me you will love yourself first before you attempt to love another person.

Promise me that you will be patient when it comes to finding true love. Promise me you'll trust in me and believe that I will deliver when the time is right.

Now let's try this again shall we.

RESURRECTION

I opened my eyes not knowing what happened. I started gasping for air, but was unable to get it. Every time I attempted to breathe it felt like my lungs were being lacerated by small pieces of glass. The pain was excruciating yet unbearable. I began to cry out for help, but nobody was around. My head was spinning, my vision was blurry along with the taste of metal on my tongue. After 5 or so minutes of trying to figure out how I got myself in such a predicament I started to hear sirens coming my way. My car was resting on its side limiting my ways of egress. With the small percentage of strength I had left in my body I tried punching the windshield as hard as I could, but nothing happened. That one punch knocked all the wind out of my lungs. I was too weak to move a second time.

Shortly after my body shut down completely the firefighters arrived with all their heavy-duty equipment ready to extricate me. I was amazed that it only took them a few minutes to free me from my car. I was so grateful that somebody found me. Once the firefighters extricated me, they placed me onto the stretcher and rolled me to the medic. I was then taken to the nearest hospital for treatment.

News Reporter: Good afternoon everyone Valerie Moore here with channel 5 news and we're back on scene of a motor vehicle collision on freeway 101. It appears the man who was pronounced dead on arrival is now alert and oriented and being treated by EMS personnel. There is no information on his condition at this time, but it's good to hear that everyone survived this devastating accident. I'm Valerie Moore with channel 5 news saying so long and to remain safe when driving on busy roads.

To Be Continued...

ACKNOWLEDGEMENTS

Dear Readers…

First off I want to thank God for allowing me to bring something that's so raw and beautiful to life. I want to thank my family/friends for sticking with me and believing in me through this entire process of writing this book. I also would like to thank my uncle Demetre Williams for his outstanding work on the book illustrations. He worked very hard bringing my imagination to life. I hope you all learned something from "A Night At The Diner" and to not repeat the same mistakes that I've made. I hope you all enjoyed reading this book as much as I enjoyed writing it. See you all again when Aiden returns!

With Love,
Cameron Pendleton

ABOUT THE AUTHOR

Readers will find interest in his unique voice as an author due to his authentic phraseology.

Printed in the United States
by Baker & Taylor Publisher Services